THIS WALKER BOOK BELONGS TO:

For Geraldine, Joe, Naomi, Eddie, Laura and Isaac
M.R.

For Elaine, Charlotte and Nicola
A.R.

First published 1990 by Walker Books Ltd
87 Vauxhall Walk, London SE11 5HJ

This edition including DVD published 2007

4 6 8 10 9 7 5

Text © 1990 Michael Rosen
Illustrations © 1990 Arthur Robins

The right of Michael Rosen and Arthur Robins
to be identified as author and illustrator respectively of this
work has been asserted by them in accordance with
the Copyright, Designs and Patents Act 1988

This book has been typeset in New Century Schoolbook

Printed in China

British Library Cataloguing in Publication Data:
a catalogue record for this book is available from the
British Library

ISBN 978-1-4063-0828-0

www.walkerbooks.co.uk

Little Rabbit Foo Foo

retold by

Michael Rosen

illustrated by

Arthur Robins

WALKER BOOKS
AND SUBSIDIARIES

LONDON · BOSTON · SYDNEY · AUCKLAND

Little Rabbit Foo Foo

riding through the forest,

scooping up the field mice

and bopping them on the head.

Down came the Good Fairy
and said, "Little Rabbit Foo Foo,
I don't like your attitude,
scooping up the field mice
and bopping them on the head.
I'm going to give you three
chances to change, and if you
don't, I'm going to turn you
into a goonie."

Little Rabbit Foo Foo
riding through the forest,

scooping up the wriggly worms
and bopping them on the head.

Down came the Good Fairy

and said, "Little Rabbit Foo Foo,
I don't like your attitude,
scooping up the wriggly worms
and bopping them on the head.
You've got two chances to change,
and if you don't, I'm going to
turn you into a goonie."

Little Rabbit Foo Foo
riding through the forest,
scooping up the tigers
and bopping them on the head.

Down came the Good Fairy
and said, "Little Rabbit Foo Foo,
I don't like your attitude,
scooping up the tigers
and bopping them on the head.

"You've got one chance left to change,
and if you don't, I'm going to
turn you into a goonie."

Little Rabbit Foo Foo
riding through the forest,
scooping up the goblins

and bopping them on the head.

Down came the Good Fairy
and said, "Little Rabbit Foo Foo,
I don't like your attitude,
scooping up the goblins
and bopping them on the head.

"You've got no chances left, so I'm
going to turn you into a goonie."

WALKER BOOKS is the world's leading

independent publisher of children's books.

Working with the best authors and illustrators

we create books for all ages, from babies

to teenagers – books your child will

grow up with and always remember. So…

FOR THE BEST CHILDREN'S BOOKS,
LOOK FOR THE BEAR